THE WINDFALL

CHRISTOPHER MILNE

The Windfall

A Fable

Wood engravings by
Kenneth Lindley

METHUEN

FOR LESLEY
who shares with me
(among so many other things)
my mistrust of Adam
and my faith in Eve

By the same author

The Enchanted Places
The Path Through The Trees
The Hollow On The Hill

First published in 1985 by
Methuen London Ltd
11 New Fetter Lane, London EC4P 4EE
Text copyright © 1985 Christopher Milne
Illustrations copyright © 1985 Kenneth Lindley

British Library Cataloguing in Publication Data

Milne, Christopher
  The windfall.
  I. Title
  823'.914[F]   PR6063.137/

  ISBN 0-413-58960-9

Designed by James Campus

Printed and bound in Great Britain by
Robert Hartnoll (1985) Ltd

The Lord God created Man
in his own image and said:
'Be fruitful and increase,
fill the earth and subdue it,
rule over the fish in the sea,
the birds of heaven
and every living thing
that moves upon the earth.'

1

Then the Lord God planted a garden in Eden away to the east, and there he put the man whom he had formed.

The Lord God made trees spring from the ground, all trees pleasant to look at and good for food; and in the middle of the garden he set the tree of life and the tree of the knowledge of good and evil.

He told the man, 'You may eat from every tree in the garden, but not from the tree of the knowledge of good and evil.'

Then the Lord God said, 'It is not good for man to be alone. I will provide a partner for him.' And he made him a wife.

EVE went into her garden. She had spent the day working. She had been along the edge of the forest to gather food. She had penetrated a little way under the trees to collect fallen sticks for her fire. She had returned home to prepare meat for their evening meal. She had fastened a new handle to an axe and resharpened the tip of one of Adam's spears. Then she had gone to the place where the nut trees grew and gathered some of the long, thin, straight wands that came up each year and these she had begun to weave into baskets. And now, having worked hard, she was going to enjoy the last few rays of the evening sunshine. It was autumn. The long stems of the grasses were turning brown and the berries on her trees were red.

Eve loved her garden. She had made it herself. That is to say she had made it without Adam's help. The flowers and bushes and trees that grew there had mostly put themselves there. And the birds and butterflies and other insects that came there came because they wanted to. She couldn't take credit for that. But there was quite a lot she had done, more perhaps than Adam suspected. She had trimmed the bushes when they became too big. She had made paths leading to the various places where she liked to sit. She had hollowed out these places so that they were smooth to lie in and sheltered from the wind. And then there were her flowers.

Some, like the grasses and bushes, had always been growing there; but there were others that she had first encountered on her expeditions to the forest in search of food. She had picked little bunches and brought them back and pushed them into the soft, moist earth. For a day or two they had stayed fresh and given her pleasure; then they had faded. They had never lasted as long as those that grew there naturally.

One day, however, stooping to pick a flower, she had accidentally pulled it up by the root; and when she had planted *this* in the earth (not knowing at all what to expect) she had been delighted to find that it not only survived for much longer but that new blossoms came. So it seemed that if she scooped deeply enough and pulled very carefully, it was possible to gather the entire plant; and this could be moved to another place where it would then continue to grow.

This was a great discovery and from then on, whenever she went walking, she would carry with her a special stick, and if she came upon a new flower she would ease it out of the ground and bring it home. Sometimes she was successful; sometimes not. Sometimes the roots went too deep and broke. Sometimes there was scarcely a root at all. Sometimes, though she seemed to have succeeded, the flower was not happy and drooped its head and died. Or it would survive for a while and then vanish away. Only one flower was always easy to dig up and always happy when moved. It was a little yellow flower that came every spring. Indeed it seemed grateful to Eve for bringing it into her garden, and, as if to thank her, would put on an extra burst of blossoms as soon as it had settled into its new home. And it would reappear year after year, always coming into bloom earlier and staying in bloom later than its fellows in the forest.

Some of her successes, she had to admit, were accidental. On one occasion she had brought home some twigs that were just coming into leaf and which she thought would look gay in a pot by their bed. But as she had not wanted to go inside just yet, she had pushed them into the ground to keep them fresh. Then Adam had come home rather earlier than usual and she had forgotten about them, so that it was not until many days later that she had rediscovered them; and to her great surprise they were now in fullest leaf. She had pulled one of the twigs out of the ground and found it had grown tiny threads of root.

This was another big discovery; for cutting twigs was very much easier than finding seedlings. But she could not persuade every tree to behave in this way.

Eve had not given individual names to every flower or tree or bird or other creature that lived in her garden. She knew them by sight, recognising them when she met them again. She could picture them in her mind, and that was enough. She didn't talk about them to Adam; for he would not have been particularly interested.

Their daily life had recently changed. There had been a time when they had found all they had needed within their garden, and they had shared the work of gathering it. But as time went by the garden seemed to be providing less – or was it that they were wanting more? – and so they had ranged further afield. Or rather it was Adam who ranged. Eve preferred to stay nearer home and prepare whatever it was that he brought back from his expeditions. It might be a fruit from some distant tree, or it might be some wild creature, a bird or an animal, that he had pursued and caught.

Then when they were together again he could tell her of his adventures. He liked to do this. He liked boasting of his triumphs and he was proud of his strength and his skill. Eve thought him very brave and very wonderful and she loved listening to him. But it made her feel glad she had not been with him. The forest frightened her. It was so different from her garden.

She stretched herself out on the grass beneath the large tree in whose shade her spring flowers grew in such abundance. Adam would be home very soon now. The sun was low, its rays coming in under the branches of the tree. Soon it would drop behind the hill. There were not many flowers at this time of year. Those still alive were tall, some almost as tall as she was, holding their heads above the surrounding grass. The autumn gales had not yet come to lay them all flat.

A bird cried urgently as it flew low over the tops of the bushes, a blackbird shouting its usual evening message. What was it saying? She wished she could understand it. Another bird, little bigger than an insect, flung her a string of defiance at the top of its voice, then popped into a hole in the bank and vanished.

The butterflies that had been so busy all day among the few remaining flowers had gone off to wherever butterflies spend the night. Only the small blue ones could now be seen. For they slept, wings folded above their bodies, clinging to the tops of the tallest grasses. Before going inside with Adam on his return, she liked to count them on her fingers and then wish them all goodnight.

Eve looked up into the branches of the tree. This was her favourite tree. It was large and spreading. The lowest branches were within reach and it was possible to scramble up into them. From there on the going was easier. The branches above were smaller, making them good to grip, and they were closer together; and soon she could be as high as it was safe to go. Sometimes she would be up in her tree when Adam came home and she could watch him looking for her. Then she would call very gently. 'Adam!' He would hear her and look round, searching. Where was she? 'Adam. Look upwards.' Ah, there she was. Their eyes would meet and they would laugh.

She had another reason for liking this particular tree: in the spring it was covered with flowers. Other trees came into flower but none had such magnificent blossoms. The flowers came before the leaves. Clusters of pink buds; then white blossoms; then the petals falling like snow. After that came the leaves to give welcome shade throughout the summer. Finally in the autumn came the fruits, larger by far than the berries on the other trees, large and round and red and shining, like the setting sun on a misty evening.

They were bright red now and they were beginning to fall.

Thump! One landed close behind her. She raked through the grass with her fingers and came upon a little cluster of them huddled together. She hardly knew which were the more beautiful, the white flowers in the spring or the red fruits in the autumn. The smaller birds and insects seemed to prefer the flowers, while the larger birds preferred the fruits.

She was reclining on her elbow holding one of the fruits in her hand. It fitted snugly into her palm and she enjoyed the sensation of holding it. She gazed at it thoughtfully. Once, a long time ago, when she was up in the tree scrambling from branch to branch, daring herself to go a little higher, she had picked one of these fruits and had nibbled it, pretending that she was a bird. It was hard and it tasted very sharp and unpleasant and it made her mouth feel dry. She had told Adam and he had been very angry and had said that the Lord God had forbidden them to eat the fruit from that particular tree. She must never do it again. 'Not even when they are red?' she had asked. 'That is when the birds eat them. May we not eat them too? Are they not good for us?' But he had answered only that it was forbidden.

Eve looked again at the apple in her hand. For indeed it was an apple. She pressed it with her thumb. It was soft and her pressure left a small dent. She noticed a place where the skin was missing and the flesh was mottled brown and white. A bird had found it first. She held it up to the sky: red against blue. She tried holding it up against the sun, but the sun dazzled her. She balanced it on her thigh. Then she picked it up once more, holding it by the stalk as the tree had held it and swinging it to and fro.

Then at last a voice in her ear said 'Eat it!' and she ate.

It was the voice of the serpent that had spoken. She knew at once that she had been tempted, that she had succumbed and had done something that one day she might bitterly regret. All this she knew but at the same time she was overwhelmed by the taste of the apple she had eaten. It was like nothing she had ever eaten before. Its white flesh was firm, yet where her teeth had entered, the juice had spurted and flowed over her tongue. It was sweet yet also sour, a perfect blend of the two, to which, after she had swallowed, was added a very slight hint of bitterness. She ate it all without a pause, not even to reject the pips and core. And as she finished the last mouthful she caught sight of Adam coming up the path towards her.

There was still a chance. She could have kept her secret to herself. But the experience had been so wonderful that the discovery had to be shared.

Poor Adam! The sack he was carrying had little in it. He had had an unsuccessful day and he was hot and tired and very thirsty and in a bad humour. With scarcely a thought he seized the apple that Eve held out to him and devoured it ravenously. Then, without speaking, he searched the grass and found another and ate it slowly, deliberately and – it seemed to Eve – almost defiantly.

Then he sat silent, staring straight ahead of him.

Eve felt frightened. 'They are so good,' she said in a whisper. 'It cannot be wrong to eat them . . . Adam, it *cannot* be wrong.'

He looked at her. He too seemed suddenly afraid.

'Adam, come closer to me.' And she held out her hand to him. But he continued to sit apart and stare at her.

'What are you thinking?' But he only shook his head.

The sun had gone behind the hill and a sudden needle of wind pricked her and made her shiver.

She stood up. 'Let's go in now. It's getting cold and you are hungry.'

'No,' said Adam. 'Not yet. I must think.'

He rose slowly to his feet and looked up into the tree.

'So many,' he said, almost as if he regretted their abundance.

'They will not harm us?' asked Eve, going towards him. 'They are not poisonous?'

Poisonous? It was a strange word.

'No,' he replied. 'They are not poisonous. That I now know.'

'You thought they were? That was why we couldn't eat them?' she asked, hoping he might say 'Yes'. But he only shook his head again.

'Look,' he said. He emptied his sack on the ground and a few small green fruits rolled out. They too were apples – of a kind. 'That's all there were. That's all I could find. There were enough on the tree when I last went, but they were not ripe. Today they were all gone – all but these few.'

'Who took them?'

'How should I know? I wasn't there to watch . . . If only all our food grew *here* where we *could* watch it and protect it and tend it . . . Out there it's so scattered. . . .'

And then quite suddenly the idea came to him.

In later years, as she listened to Adam telling his story to his descendants – listening in silence as became a dutiful wife – it would make Eve smile to herself that somehow he always forgot to mention that it was *she* who had first discovered the possibility of digging plants out of the ground and moving them to another place, and *she* who discovered that trees and bushes could sometimes be persuaded to grow where you wanted them to grow by pushing little bits of them into the earth. Yes, of course, it needed a clever, practical man like Adam to make use of her discovery, to see that if flowers could be moved so too could food plants. And so too, quite possibly, could animals. And of course it was Adam's idea that led to the great change in their lives. No. Even that was not quite true. For this change would have occurred in any case, as a result of her eating the apple. If she had never been tempted, never disobeyed, would Adam's wonderful idea have had such consequences? How complicated it all was!

Eve never managed to puzzle it out to her complete satisfaction. Better, therefore, to let Adam tell the story in his own way. The thing had happened whatever might have been its causes and origins and whoever might fairly claim the credit – or take the blame – and whether it was chance or the deep workings of inevitability that lay at the back of it all.

This at least was certain: they had spent the rest of that evening in long discussion, the red apples and the green apples lying side by side on the ground quite forgotten.

'Just think,' said Adam, 'how much easier it would be if *all* our food grew here where I could look after it.'

'It did once, you remember.'

'It could again. I'd have to get rid of everything we didn't need: all the things we can't eat.'

'You can't eat my flowers,' said Eve defensively. 'Would you get rid of them? They're not useful but they are pretty . . . At least I think so.'

'Food must come first,' said Adam firmly.

He walked a little way and Eve hurried after him. It was a wonderful idea but somehow it frightened her. She had been so happy the way things were, even though in winter they had often gone hungry. It had been hard for Adam, it is true. But he had seemed contented. He enjoyed his expeditions into the forest and his adventures there. He enjoyed his hunting. Would he not miss this if he were now to spend all his time in the garden? And what would *she* do? Would he want her to help him? She wondered if she would be allowed to keep her own little corner the way she liked it.

'Please, Adam. This bit here, where my yellow flowers grow and where it is so pleasant to sit. You could sit here too after you had done your work. You'd have more time for sitting. . . . I like just being with them,' she added, almost to herself. 'Not *doing* anything – though I may perhaps pick a few

and bring them inside. Not even looking at them – though I sometimes like to get very close to them and stare deep into their hearts. Just being with them: feeling that they and I are sharing something together, though I don't know what it is. Perhaps it's the world we share, or our small bit of it. And then if I sit still perhaps I will see a fly or some other tiny creature, and he too will come into my world and share it with me.'

Adam, who hadn't been listening, didn't answer. His mind was so full of his wonderful new idea, this idea of not taking the world as it was but of making it the way you wanted it to be. Already in imagination he was digging at the grass, clearing the soil, cutting and burning, making all ready for the new plants he would be bringing in from the forest. Why had he never thought of doing this before? The first thing for Eve to do would be to collect all the fallen apples before the birds got them. Of course it would all take time, years perhaps. He would have to experiment, find out which things were easiest to move and what was the best way of moving them.

He climbed the hill. Yes, Eve had certainly made it very pleasant up here. He came to a tree he did not remember having seen before, a tree now heavy with strangely-coloured fruit. The tree was large and the fruit out of reach. Perhaps that was why Eve had never picked them. He didn't think they had been forbidden.

As he stood looking up into the branches Eve came and joined him.

'It's pretty,' she said. 'Especially in the spring. But I don't think you can eat them.'

'I'd like to try one,' he answered. 'We didn't know about the apples until we had tried them.'

'Not now,' said Eve. 'We've done enough for one day. I'll see if I can reach you one tomorrow.'

She smiled, a little sadly, and put an arm round his waist.

2

The Lord God said, 'The man has become like one of us knowing good from evil. What if he now reaches out his hand and takes fruit from the tree of life also, eats it and lives for ever?'

So to the man he said: 'You have listened to your wife and have eaten from the tree which I forbade you. So now with labour must you win your food all the rest of your life.'

And to the woman he said: 'From hence forward your husband shall rule over you.'

And he drove them out of the Garden.

Then Adam lay with his wife and she conceived and gave birth to Cain; and afterwards she had another child, his brother Abel.

Abel became a shepherd and Cain a tiller of the soil.

THE boys had been fighting again. It seemed to Eve they were always fighting – and about such little things. They would be working together happily, seemingly the best of friends, and then one would say something, and the other would take offence . . . and they would be off. They were so prickly, so easily offended, each so jealous of the other's achievements. She had talked about it to Adam but, strangely, it didn't seem to worry him. 'A little competition does them good,' he had laughed. 'That's the way to get on.' And certainly they had got on since leaving Eden. Eve couldn't deny that.

Yes, they had left: the Lord God had decreed it. Eve was sad to go. She had loved it there. Adam was less sad. He could see that the garden was not really suitable. It was too confined, too perfect. It would have been wrong to try and change it: here he agreed with Eve. What he needed was a wilderness that he could clear and shape and make exactly as he wanted it to be. The place they had come to suited him perfectly.

Adam was immensely proud of what he had done in the short time they had been here. 'Come and look,' he would say to Eve when the day's work was over. And they would go out together and he would show her and she would admire; and then he would tell her of his plans. He was always so full of plans, of dreams for the future: new tools he was experimenting with, new crops he hoped to plant, new ways of protecting his stock, new places where he might extend his land.

His stock, *his* crops, *his* land. This was the great difference since they had left Eden. There they had been hunters. Now they were farmers. Or rather Adam was a farmer and so were the boys. It was man's work. She was . . . What? A farmer's wife, she supposed. 'His', 'Ours', 'Mine'. These were words they had scarcely used in the old days. In the forest things didn't belong to you. They didn't belong to anybody. They were just there and you took what you wanted, what you could catch or what you could find. When you had caught it and brought it home, then of course it was yours. Who else could it belong to? And then you ate it and that made it still more yours. But here on the farm there was, it seemed, a need to claim ownership, and so you said, 'This is mine.' You said it confidently, proudly. But sometimes you said it challengingly, as if expecting someone to dispute it. This too she had mentioned to Adam; for it made her uneasy, this new relationship with the world around them. But again Adam had laughed at her fears. 'Weren't they "your" flowers that you used to dig up and bring back to "your" garden?' And she had to admit that this was partly true.

The great difference, she decided, was that when they had been hunters they had lived from day to day – or very nearly. When they had wanted something, they had gone out and found it and then straight away they had used it. Sometimes, it is true, they had watched fruit ripening and had said to each other, 'Next week we will come and pick it.' But they had never thought of the fruit as belonging to them until it had

21

been gathered and brought home. They had not laid claim to it while it was still green. And if, in the interval, some other creature took it – well – they would probably find more elsewhere. But now that they were farmers Adam worked as much for the future as for the present. Reaping: that was for the present; but sowing: that was for the future. And there was a long and anxious period between the two when he had to protect his unfinished work until the fruits of his labour could be realised.

Nor was that the only difference. Because in Eden they had lived from day to day, eating the food they had brought home, burning the fuel they had gathered, there had been little left over at the end of the year to show for the year's work. But now each day something of the day's work survived and was added to what had survived from the previous day, and this brought steady change, steady progress. Eve knew that Adam found this immensely satisfying and that it gave him tremendous pleasure to go out first thing in the morning and stand and survey what he had done the day before, what he had achieved to date. The Lord God when he had made the world had doubtless felt the same. He had looked on his work and seen that it was good. Day by day he had added to it, and day by day it had become more perfect.

That was the great blessing of their new life; and even though it was a blessing that fell mainly upon Adam and the boys, Eve was grateful for it. It made Adam so happy, so proud of what he had done, so eager for Eve's admiration, so full of plans. He used to say that before going to sleep he would lie awake and in his head dream, minute by minute, his next day's tasks. He said that this not only doubled the pleasure, but that in his dreaming he could experiment and so discover the best way of doing things.

This made Eve smile. 'How you do love work!' Well, if he enjoyed it, there could be no harm in it. And certainly they

were warmer and better fed than they had ever been. Yes, here indeed was a blessing – despite the quarrelling that it so often seemed to provoke. But alongside it went something that distressed her.

In the old days they had sought what they had wanted where it was to be found. They had gone hunting. Not necessarily together, of course, for Adam liked to penetrate deep into the forest where the wild animals lived. He loved these expeditions, revelling in the chase, exulting in his triumph when with a well-hurled spear he had brought down his quarry. Eve's arms were not made for throwing nor were her legs made for running. And though she was happy to cook what was already dead, she disliked killing and she disliked even more to see creatures die. Yet she too in her way was a hunter. Her expeditions took her only to the fringe of the forest. Here she would hunt for berries and nuts and leaves and the eggs of birds. She knew – it seemed she had always known – where these things were to be found. Not all plants were good to eat of course. You had to know what you were looking for. Eve knew. It didn't matter to her that there were a lot of other things that she was not looking for. She let them be.

But now it did matter. Now it seemed there were bad things as well as good, and the bad things could not be ignored. They had to be fought and destroyed. As hunters they needed to know only what was good. As a farmer Adam had to know also what was bad.

Eve disliked the idea that something could be bad, a bird or an insect or an animal or a plant with a pretty flower. And she disliked the idea of destroying something because it was bad. You could kill a thing if you were going to use it in some way: you could kill it for its goodness. But it was altogether different to kill it because you did *not* want it.

Adam couldn't see this. 'Weeds and pests,' he had said.

(And the very words were new: there had been no weeds or pests either in the forest or in the garden.) 'Weeds and pests have to be destroyed if we want anything to eat. I'm not going to labour day after day clearing the soil, ploughing and sowing, only to watch the birds come down and help themselves to my corn when it's ripe. I'm not working for them. I'm working for us.'

He was quite right of course. It was *his* corn from the moment the seed was in the ground. His ground. His corn. But it was not just that. For Eve had noticed – and this greatly troubled her – that he was no reluctant fighter, doing what he had to do because he had to do it. On the contrary, he enjoyed it. He relished it. Sometimes, in the old days, when he had come home with an animal and Eve had praised him, he had seemed dissatisfied. Eve, puzzled, had asked him what was wrong and he had given the curious reason that he had caught it too easily. It had never worried Eve that she had found her plants too easily. Quite the reverse! But Adam liked what he called 'a good chase'. He would swear that the meat from a creature that had 'put up a good fight' tasted the sweetest – though Eve herself could never detect any difference.

Adam liked a fight not just for the meal that followed it but for the pleasure of testing his skill and his strength against 'a worthy adversary'. He welcomed the challenge and he exulted in the victory. Though he had never admitted as much, Eve believed that there were occasions when, in the heat of the chase, intoxicated with success, he had killed more creatures than he had been able to carry home and had left the others where they had fallen.

So perhaps it was not altogether surprising that he should now welcome – yes, actually welcome – the attacks that were made on his crops and his sheep. They challenged his authority. They tested his skills. They brought him the 'victories' that so elated him. But Eve, out walking and coming across the body of a dead wolf, or a heap of withered plants – 'weeds' she supposed – would be saddened.

This difference between them explained why, though she had enjoyed her share of the hunting, she could never be a farmer. She was grateful to the Lord God for her days in Eden. She herself could have stayed there for ever. But perhaps for Adam's sake they had to leave. And so perhaps the greatest gift the Lord God could have given them when the time came for their departure lay within the apple they had eaten: a knowledge of good *and evil*. For if there would be enemies opposing their new way of life, surely they needed to know them.

At the time it had puzzled her that God should have said to Adam, 'With labour shall you win your food.' For she had imagined that, once they had found and made a new home for themselves, life would be easier. She had been wrong. It was harder. Yet was it not also in some ways better, more rewarding?

She had been puzzled, too, that God had said to her that Adam would rule over her; for in the Garden neither had wished to 'rule over' the other. This too she could now understand. It was a man's world they had entered, a world in which his love of risk, of adventure and of success, of challenge, of struggle and of victory would find all the opportunities it needed – until in the end, she supposed, he would be lord of the entire world and every plant and every animal that he had allowed to survive would owe him allegiance.

Eve sighed. It was harvest time. The autumn always made her sad, though for Adam and the boys it was the culmination of the year's work, a time of triumph and of celebration. They would celebrate as they always did, with a feast. Abel would bring a lamb, Cain some corn. It was good that they had agreed to divide the work in this way, Abel looking after

the sheep, Cain the crops. It helped to keep them apart and so gave them less cause to quarrel with each other.

She heard their voices and the sound of their footsteps and went outside to greet them.

3

Cain said to his brother, 'Let us go into the open country.' And while he was there he attacked his brother and murdered him.

Then Adam lay with his wife again and she bore a son and named him Seth.

THE avenue was Adam's pride. He had begun planting it when Seth had been born. He had started it at their doorstep and each year he had added a few trees to it, carrying it forwards, absolutely straight, across the valley towards the wild country that at that time lay at the far end. The trees had come from a nearby forest. Adam had found them and dug them up, beeches mostly, but also an occasional oak. They had been waist high when he had moved them and for several years they had not grown at all. In the spring new leaves had come; in the autumn they had turned brown and the late winter gales had finally blown them away just as the new buds were fattening up. The leaves of the oak were a different shape from those of the beech but apart from that there was little to distinguish the one from the other.

Then one year, in the early summer, they noticed a change. New shoots, the length of a hand, had appeared almost over-night on the first trees Adam had planted. Thereafter, each year, as he added to his avenue, so, following behind him but keeping their distance, another group of the older trees would start to grow; and it was in this annual growth that the different personalities of the two kinds of tree first emerged.

In this they were like human children which, all babies at first, later separate into boys and girls. So in their annual growth beeches became feminine, oaks masculine. Eve would refer to them as 'your boys' and 'my girls'.

'Look at your boys now,' she would say. 'Bristling with a hundred spears. Don't they frighten you?' There was indeed something aggressive about the way the young oaks grew, their new shoots, straight as arrows, stabbing in all direc-tions. How different were the beeches, whose delicate new growth, like the waters of a fountain, arched up, curved over and drooped towards the ground. There they hung, graceful and modest, for over a month, then slowly stiffened and straightened until they were pointing skywards.

The avenue marked a new beginning in their lives. For, with Abel's death and Cain's departure, Adam's first high hopes of success had crashed to the ground. It was not just the sudden and tragic loss of two children. Children come and go. This they could have borne. What frightened them was the effect on their surroundings.

If in Eden there had suddenly been two mouths fewer there would have been more food for the two that survived. But in their new life it was the opposite. With Cain and Abel gone, there was not more to eat but less – alarmingly less. Over the years the three men had pushed forward the boundaries of their land, bringing more and more of the wild country under cultivation.

Adam had imagined that, where he had fought and defeated the enemy, he would remain for ever the undisputed victor. It had not occurred to him that the wilderness, now held at bay only by himself, would so fiercely fight back and so quickly recapture lost territory.

Now more than ever did he appreciate the truth of the Lord God's words: 'With labour shall you win your food.' The thorns and the thistles, more savage than he had ever known them before, were all around him. Eve had been near to despair and had begged Adam to return to Eden so that they might throw themselves on the mercy of the Lord God and beg to be readmitted. But Adam, proud and determined, refused to surrender. He decided how much land he would need for the two of them, which were the most convenient pastures, which soil was the most fertile, and this he defended, driving in stakes and piling up a rampart of earth and stones to form a perimeter defence. The rest he abandoned.

Ten years after Seth's arrival he was able once more to push forward and regain a little of what he had lost. More sons and daughters quickly followed, and all, as they grew up, moved away across the plain, clearing the wilderness and establishing farmsteads of their own.

Generation after generation the farmsteads moved eastwards, and, as they spread out across the plain, so the techniques of agriculture improved. But always there were battles: these were unending. Man having once put his hand to the plough could never again rest.

Adam left the young to their fighting. He had reached middle age. His great battles were now over. He and the rest of nature had come to accept each other's existence, and a truce had been established. He continued to farm but in a smaller, gentler way, a few sheep and a few crops. If extra help were needed, then one or other of his sons would come over to lend a hand.

Eve too had established a truce. For, yes, she too had become a fighter, though a much gentler and more reluctant one than Adam. She did not work in the fields except at harvest time. She and her daughters had enough to do in and around their home, a home which they shared, inevitably, with a host of other creatures.

Some of these had been in residence before she and Adam had arrived and had subsequently adapted themselves to the presence of humans. Others, approving of the alterations being made, had moved in. For there is throughout nature, from the lowliest plant to man himself, a constant coming and going as circumstances change.

Eve did not divide her fellow residents into 'good' and 'evil' but she did give a warmer welcome to some than to others. It was not just that she favoured those plants and animals that she and Adam could eat or that served some other practical purpose. Some creatures she liked simply for themselves, for no better reason than that they seemed to like her and be happy in the company of each other. She came to regard them as part of her family.

Others she liked because she had known them as a child and they had established a special place in her affections. It was soon after the birth of Seth that she had begun to feel this nostalgia for her first garden, and she had tried to introduce some of the flowers that had grown there into her new garden. But she was not always successful. The newcomers were often unhappy. The older residents resented their intrusion. Eve got angry with them and Adam was amused to hear her referring to them as 'weeds'. After a short while the attempt was abandoned.

Thus Eve in her home and Adam in his fields reached in the end a stable relationship with their surroundings. Their arrival had been followed by years in which great changes had occurred. But these changes were now over and a new pattern had replaced the old. Yet though in temperament husband and wife were now much closer than they had been at the start, a difference still remained, a difference which, for better or for worse, was always to distinguish man from woman.

Then came the visit to Jared.

People in those times lived a great deal longer than they do today. Jared was then around sixty and still had another hundred years to wait before his first son was born. Adam was his great-great-great-grandfather and had just reached his five hundredth birthday.

Their journey across the plain was almost the first time they had left their own valley and certainly by far the longest distance they had ever attempted. Travelling outwards they were thus seeing, largely for the first time, a pageant of four hundred years of human progress, and it took them into a land very different from the one they knew so well.

For Adam it was a fascinating experience, passing through a landscape that was perpetually changing, trying to understand the new methods that were being used, the new tools, marvelling at the new buildings where people lived together in such large communities. Eve, though she had a mother's pride in the achievements of her children and her children's children – in the sheer numbers of them that now filled the plain – felt uneasy at what they had done. It was all so frighteningly different.

Where would it end? There had been much to admire certainly, but they had passed a place where something had clearly gone wrong. The landscape was ravaged and naked. Nothing grew there – just tree stumps, bare earth, stagnant pools of water and what looked like the decaying remnants of abandoned buildings now little more than sad heaps of stones. What exactly had happened? The answers she had been given were evasive.

On their return journey the pageant was reversed: they were travelling backwards through time. They were discussing what they had seen and Eve's anxiety about the future was weighing on her. They had again passed the place that had so frightened her on the outward journey and it had frightened her even more seeing it a second time. She was convinced that something evil had happened, and on top of this was a conviction that in some way she had been to blame.

This feeling of guilt had assailed her once before – when Abel had been killed – and it had taken many years to recover from it. Now it assailed her again. For surely all evil, all suffering lay at her door. She had disobeyed the command of the Lord God. It was true that the serpent had tempted her. But the choice had been hers. And not only had she disobeyed; she had persuaded Adam to do likewise. She was thus doubly guilty. That single act of disobedience had totally changed the pattern of all their lives. All the sorrows of the world had their origin in what she had done.

'It's all my fault,' she cried.

'What is?' said Adam. Their thoughts had diverged since last they had spoken to each other.

'Evil,' said Eve simply.

'Then Good too,' answered Adam. 'We saw plenty of that.'

But Eve was not so easily consoled and Adam tried another argument.

'You remember the wound on Jared's hand that you helped to wash, and how he told us it came from a tool he had been using? He showed me that tool. He had made it himself. It was a wonderful thing. Sharper and better than anything I have ever been able to make. Now tell me, was that tool evil to have injured the hand that held it? Or was Jared wicked to have invented it? If you invent tools that make work easier, you must accept the risk that they can do greater damage.'

'I don't see what that has to do with disobedience,' Eve said.

Adam was silent for a little. Then he tried again.

'When Seth was a child we told him that, though he might go down to the stream, he must never cross over to the other side unless he was with one of us. We made that rule, not because there were greater dangers on the far side of the stream, nor because there was any particular risk that he might slip and drown in trying to get across, but simply because it made it easier for us to look after him. If we had allowed him his freedom to wander where he pleased, he might well have wandered too far and got lost or met with some accident and we might never have found him. I chose the stream as his limit for no other reason than that it made a clear boundary between what was permitted and what was forbidden. If he chose to cross, I would punish him: that he knew.

'But I knew – and he didn't – that one day he *would* cross. *And I would be glad.* I would be glad because it would prove that he was no longer a child dependent upon his father for protection but a man dependent only upon himself. I could have said, ''Today you are a man. Now you have my permission.'' But I preferred him to make the discovery for himself. I preferred that the time and the decision should be his, not mine. You do not become a man because your father says you are one, but because you feel yourself to be one.

'That it how it was with Seth, and it was exactly the same with us when we were children and lived in Eden, and the Lord God was our father. He provided for us. Our food was there, all around us, and we helped ourselves to it, while he watched over us. Then when we were strong enough to be independent of him, we proved it to him by breaking his command. And the apple which had been forbidden to us when we were children became his great gift to us, the gift that enabled us to survive on our own.'

'But I never wanted to leave my garden,' cried Eve. 'That wasn't why I ate the apple. It was . . . I don't know . . . curiosity.'

'Nor, I think, did Seth want to leave home. But he proved to me that he was ready to go, and so I sent him away. It is right for children to leave home when they are grown up. That was our mistake with Cain and Abel: we allowed them to stay.'

'It is good of you, dear Adam, to excuse me. And perhaps the Lord God excuses me too. But I fear others may not do so. They will see it differently.'

'If things go right our children will, of course, give themselves the credit. If they go wrong they will look for others to blame. Yes, they will certainly blame us.'

They walked on in silence.

After a while Eve said: 'I was very frightened at first. Frightened of you. Did you know?'

'There were times when I was a bit frightened of myself,' answered Adam with a laugh.

'You became so different; so . . . so . . .' She sought in vain for the word. 'I didn't like that fighting. All that killing. We seemed to have so many enemies and you were so fierce.'

'I had to be,' said Adam. 'We couldn't have survived any other way.'

'I'm glad it's over now. But they are still fighting up there – Jared and the others. Does the great plain stretch for ever or does it come to an end? What happens when they reach the end? What happens on the other side?'

Adam shook his head. He had never thought of such a possibility.

They were nearing home now. The landscape was becoming more familiar. The late winter sun was level with their eyes, orange and no longer dazzling. Their elongated shadows trailed behind them. It had suddenly turned cold after a day of rare warmth. Soon afterwards the track went downhill. They were entering their valley at last and the sun, having guided them across the plain, its duty done, now slipped quietly behind the far horizon.

The valley beneath them lay in shadow, a monochrome of black and grey, but the sky was still alive with colour from deepest crimsons to palest greens. As they made their way down the hill so, one by one, the valley trees seemed to rise up out of the darkness to greet their return. One by one they thrust their leafless heads through the rim of the sleeping world, and as they moved upwards into the sky so they caught in the network of their branches a million fragments of colour, a shoal of rubies and emeralds and amethysts and sapphires. Many thousands of years later men would celebrate this evening flowering of winter trees in the stained glass windows of their churches. But though they were able to capture the colours, the individual personalities of the trees themselves eluded them.

These were Adam's trees. He had planted them, every one. He knew them as he knew his own children. Indeed they

were his children. And this was how he and Eve liked best to see them, naked against the winter's sky.

First to salute them was the oak with the straight trunk and the round head that stood where the track began to level out; and soon afterwards came two more solitary oaks.

'Rough old oaks,' said Eve. 'Their heads are as bristly as your beard.'

'They are men,' said Adam. 'They are my sons.'

'And the beeches are our daughters.'

Adam smiled. 'Their trunks are smooth like the body of a woman. Their branches are like a woman's arms; and their heads have a woman's hair, as fine and soft as the wind itself. They are indeed our daughters.'

'They are like us,' said Eve, 'and yet they are the opposite of us. For in winter when we need clothes to keep warm they are naked, and in the summer when we are naked they are clothed.'

'I like them naked best,' said Adam. 'I like you naked best, too. You are you when you are naked. I can see you and touch you and know you. When the trees are clothed in their leaves I can pick a leaf and say what tree it belongs to, but the leaf will tell me nothing of the nature of the tree. It is the same with clothes; they tell us who we are but not what we are.'

A group of trees, half a dozen clustering together on a little hillock, rose against the sky.

'Look at those oaks,' said Eve. 'Aren't they just like men! Six men having an argument, shouting at each other, elbowing each other, threatening each other. Look how their branches twist and stab, how they fight each other and hurt each other. Poor things! They are wounded trees.'

'Yet they survive,' said Adam, 'wounded or not.'

Another group came into view.

'There! See what a difference,' cried Eve. 'My girls. So

close to each other, so happy to be close. Each one perfect, its branches slipping through the branches of its neighbours. No fighting. Just peace and happiness.'

They had reached the avenue now and walked more slowly, arm in arm. It was darker here. The great smooth round columns of the beeches rose on either hand, one behind the other, evenly spaced, stretching away ahead of them. High above their heads each column opened out into its branches, branches that arched up and over, meeting and crossing those of its partner on the opposite side of the track and those of its neighbours on the same side.

Eve held up her arms and arched the palms of her hands towards each other so that her finger tips met and crossed.

'Look. They do it like this.' It was the attitude of prayer.

'When you planted them, did you mean it to be like this? Did you know they would grow this way and make a canopy over our heads?'

'No,' said Adam. 'They were forest trees growing wild when I found them. Trees don't grow in straight lines in the forest. I dug them up and planted them here, two and two, exactly spaced, flanking a path that was as straight as I could make it. I did it that way to show that they were now my trees growing on my land.'

'And that you were their Lord and Master?'

'Yes, and that I was their Lord and Master.'

'Are you still their Lord and Master?'

'They are taller and stronger than I am now. I think perhaps I have given them their freedom, though happily they are reluctant to leave me. I shan't drive them away.'

They had reached the end of the avenue. One solitary tree now filled the sky. It stood quite alone. It was immensely large, towering up into the sky, yet stretching its branches out horizontally on either side to give it a breadth that was greater even than its great height. This enormous head was

carried on a trunk as broad almost as it was tall. It was a giant oak.

'Adam's Oak,' said Eve. 'No mightier tree will the world ever know.'

And she touched its rough bark with her hands and knelt at its foot and rested her head against its trunk and wept.

4

After the birth of Seth Adam lived eight hundred years, and had other sons and daughters. He lived in all nine hundred and thirty years, and then he died.

When the Lord saw that man had done much evil on earth and and that his thoughts and inclinations were always evil, and that the whole world was corrupt and full of violence, he was sorry that he had made man on earth, and he was grieved at heart. He said, 'This race of men whom I have created, I will wipe them off the face of the earth.'

EVE took her largest container and went down to the stream, to the place where Adam had wedged a tree trunk between the banks and filled behind with rocks and earth to make a miniature waterfall. Behind this was a pool where, even in the driest weather, the water was always deep. Here she dipped. Then she carried her burden up the hillside.

She lived alone now. Adam had been dead many years, and the land that lay on the far side of the stream was now farmed by others.

It was midsummer. The winter had been unusually wet, the spring unusually dry. The sun shone from a cloudless sky and had been doing so day after day for an unusually long time.

Eve loved all weathers and all seasons. They were part of the living world, and the to-and-fro movement between them – from darkness to light, from new moon to full moon, from winter to summer, from east wind to west wind, from gale to calm, from rain to sunshine, from frost to thaw – was the world's breathing and showed that it was alive and in good health.

Only when the rhythm became erratic, when the world drew its breath in great spasms like a person who is ill, did she become afraid. And only when she was afraid did she begin to think of the weather as cruel.

Although there is no precise moment when the sun's kindly smile becomes a smile of cruelty, there may well be a precise moment when one becomes aware of such a change. For Eve this moment was the day she carried the water up the hillside to her grove of trees to offer it to the three young saplings she had planted there in the spring.

Eve's grove was like Adam's avenue in that it expressed, whether consciously or not, her attitude towards the living world. In later years men were to express themselves in timber and stone. She and Adam did so in trees. But whereas Adam had planted his beeches evenly spaced in two straight lines – to show, as he used to say, whose trees they were – Eve planted her grove in the more casual way that the trees themselves seemed to prefer. She had begun planting soon after Adam's death and had continued intermittently ever since: oak and ash and beech and hazel mainly, but also occasionally hawthorn and birch and field maple. The three new saplings were hawthorns.

Eve seldom visited her grove in the height of summer. She preferred it in the winter, when the trees rose naked from the naked earth, and in the spring, when the flowers made patches of colour between the trees, yellow first, then blue and finally pink. But after that came a sudden wild upsurge of green that swamped the flowers, and at that season she preferred to sit by the stream where the sheep grazed and the grass was short.

There had been no rain for so long that she had begun to fear for her three hawthorns. Newly-planted trees dislike a drought. She had been up the hill that morning to search for them, fighting her way through head-high bracken to reach them. They were indeed dry. Their leaves were hanging limply and some had already turned yellow. She was returning now with the water they so badly needed.

She began to pour it round the base of the first tree. She had imagined that because the soil here was so dry and powdery, so obviously thirsty, it would swallow the water at a gulp, and she was disconcerted to find that, so far from soaking in, it merely rolled off down the slope. She stopped pouring at once, put down her container and loosened the soil with her fingers. Then she poured again, and again the water rolled away. So she found a stick and with its help she scooped out a hollow behind the stem of the tree and brought the earth forward to form a rampart in front. The rest of her water she now poured into this hollow until it was level with the top of her rampart. Then she went down the hill to collect more water.

On her return she found the pool as deep as ever. She visited the other two trees and prepared them in the same way, excavating the soil at the back and bringing it to the front. Then she filled both hollows with water.

After a rest, for it was hot and wearying work, she visited the stream for the third time. She thought she might manage six journeys a day – two for each tree – and she hoped this might be enough to keep them alive until the rain came.

But the three water levels were unchanged. She went to the first tree, tried pouring a little more and for a moment thought it was soaking in. Then she noticed a thin trickle snaking its way through the grass between her feet. She thrust her hand down into the water and scrabbled with her fingers into the soil. She jabbed with her stick to loosen the stones. Some fragments of dust rose to the surface and were joined a moment afterwards by a tiny insect. The insect dented the surface of the water. Its legs raced but to no effect. Eve watched its futile efforts. The water was still gently girating from her work with the stick, and the insect, caught in the movement, circled the pool.

'Poor creature,' said Eve. 'My efforts are as little welcome to you as they are to my tree.' And she dipped her finger in and drew it up and it sat on her finger tip encased in a drop of water. She shook her finger and the insect vanished.

That for Eve was the day the drought began, the day the kindly sun turned cruel. Its cruelty was not directed against her personally. She had plenty to eat and plenty to drink. If she was too hot she could move into the shade or bathe herself in the stream. What pained her was the suffering she saw or imagined she saw in the other creatures, particularly the suffering of the earth itself.

To Eve the earth had always seemed alive, the living home of countless living plants and animals. Lying upon it she could feel it holding her up, powerful and reassuring beneath her body. Pressing her hands against it she could feel the living earth press back. She would explore it and caress it with her fingers. She would press her face into it and inhale its living breath.

But now and in the days that followed it hurt her to look at it, so different had it become, like a friend greatly changed through illness. It glared back at her as if it had never known her, as if it cared nothing for her, grim and unloving, locked in its own private torment.

She continued to water her three trees. A single container a day shared between them was all she could persuade them to drink, and she doubted very much whether it would be enough. There was so little she could do for the suffering earth, but to do nothing was worse. Each day she carried her water up the hillside and poured it. It became a daily ritual, a symbolic gesture that expressed her feelings of love and faith; and she found it strangely satisfying.

Then one afternoon she noticed a change. A tenseness seemed to grip the world. There were sudden rustlings, sudden puffs of wind. Birds flew from tree to tree. The sheep were unusually noisy. Towards evening the sky became slashed and streaked and smeared with strange patterns of cloud. Soon afterwards it grew very dark.

Then came the noise of the approaching storm. The wind had dropped. The waiting world held its breath in silence, and so the first sounds came from far away, a gentle hissing that grew steadily louder and louder, increasing to a roar that reached its climax with a great crash as giant hailstones hurtled out of the pitch black sky and battered the earth all round her. Eve quickly got under cover and the noise on the roof over her head was deafening.

The hailstorm died away and was followed by a steady torrent of rain. She ventured outside again and stood naked with her arms stretched up towards the sky. The rain stung her body and soaked her and washed the salt sweat from her skin. She threw back her head and shut her eyes and opened her mouth and let the rain beat upon her teeth and upon her tongue. There was so much rain that it drowned the air, making it hard to breathe. All around her came a steady roar as the water hit the earth and flattened it into submission. She stood thus, exulting, then went inside.

The rain was streaming through the roof and the floor was awash. In the darkness she sought her bed and lay down and covered herself over to wait for daylight. She was cold. She had almost forgotten what it was like to feel cold and she enjoyed the sensation. Then, pulling her coverings close over her body and over her head, she enjoyed the sensation of returning warmth. She lay awake listening to the noises that were all around her – the sudden buffetings of the wind, the creakings from the roof, the periodic slitherings and thumpings and drippings and splashings and cascadings as more and more of the roof surrendered to the storm. And twice she heard from afar a long-drawn rending, tearing, splintering crash as some hard-pressed tree succumbed to the combined onslaught of wind and water.

As soon as a faint grey daylight returned to the world she got up and went outside. Adam had built well. Only the roof had suffered; and though torrents of water were spouting from the hillside, the wall that encircled their home had not been breached. Beyond it, however, was desolation: the grass

50

flattened, trees with their branches weighed to the ground with water, leaves and broken twigs everywhere, water and earth and stones swirling and leaping down the hillside, a strong sweet smell of sap in the air, the rain as heavy as ever.

Back under cover again she noticed that as the rain dried on her body the hairs on her skin became dark brown. When she wiped herself there remained a muddy smear.

During the day the rain slackened a little, its first fury spent, and she was able to make some repairs and salvage her belongings. The following day she ventured to the stream. The bridge had vanished and she doubted if she could now get safely across.

As she stood there, something large and white came bounding down on the flood. It was a sheep. It passed beyond her reach. But even if it had been nearer she could never have checked its wild progress. And in any case it was dead.

Closer to the bank where the water travelled more slowly came a mole. It was paddling frantically, like the tiny insect she had rescued when she had been giving water to the trees, and as the eddies caught it and turned it now this way, now that, so its blind efforts would be directed sometimes towards, sometimes away from the shore. Eve reached out a hand but it eluded her and went spinning on its way.

A sheep and a mole. She wondered what had become of the people.

When she looked outside the next day she was alarmed to find that the stream had become a broad lake whose nearer shore was already climbing the hillside towards her and whose further shore was scarcely visible through the driving rain. As she stood there looking over her wall she saw a figure come down to the water's edge on the far side and appear to be staring in her direction. She waved and shouted. The figure saw her and waved back but no sound reached her.

They waved to each other for a while and Eve shouted that

she was all right. But the rain drowned her words and the wind swept the fragments away. There was nothing more they could do. The water divided them and there was no safe way across. Soon afterwards, with a final wave, the figure turned and departed.

The following day the water was so close that Eve decided she must retreat. Behind her rose the mountains. These were the mountains through which she and Adam had journeyed many hundreds of years ago when they had been driven out of Eden. They had crossed the mountains and come to the plain on whose edge they had settled and built their home. And while they had been building it – gathering stones and cutting timber and cementing and daubing with mud – they had taken shelter in a cave they had found on the mountainside. It was this cave that Eve now sought; and to her great relief, though nearly blinded by rain and low cloud, she was able to rediscover it. And it was dry and welcoming.

All that day she journeyed back and forth, carrying food and fuel, and by the evening she had moved her entire store. That night she slept well and it was already daylight when she woke. She went to the mouth of the cave and looked out. It was still raining but the cloud had lifted and the air was clearer. She could see further, and from her elevated position there was further to see.

The plain stretched away to the distant horizon. Not since that first time those many years ago had she seen it thus in all its vastness. Then it had been green and inviting. Now – she could scarcely believe what she saw: there was nothing in front of her but an unbroken expanse of water. Not a hilltop, not a treetop, not a solitary sign of life. All had been totally submerged.

At first she was too numbed with shock to be afraid or to consider what it might mean. She returned to her cave, and hardly knowing what she was doing, she set herself to make it

habitable and to sort and tidy and arrange her various belongings. She worked vigorously, keeping her back to the outside world, and when darkness came she was exhausted and ready for bed.

That night she slept restlessly, waking frequently, and, as often happens on such occasions, her dreams were vivid and more closely related to her waking thoughts than is usual. She had three dreams and when morning came at last to lighten the entrance to her cave she was able to recall them all.

In her first dream she was looking down on a great expanse of water. The water was brown and turbulent, and froth and debris floated on its surface. As she looked, a small insect rose to the surface and began paddling. It was followed by a mole, also paddling, then by a dead sheep and finally by a man. Insect, mole, sheep and man, one behind the other, three of them struggling, the fourth quietly floating, circled the water in steady procession.

Eve stretched down and tried to reach them but something restrained her. It was a tree. She was caught in the branches of a great tree. Using both hands to grip the branches below her she managed to pull herself down a little way. But by that time the procession had moved out of range.

She then saw that the water was retained along one side by a rampart of loose earth. If she could only reach this and draw her finger across it she could release the flood. Again she set to work to haul herself downwards; and when she thought she was low enough she took a firm grip with her left hand and heaved, and stretched downwards with her right, and her extended finger was just able to touch the earth. With a tremendous effort, pulling with one hand and stretching with the other, she was able to make a small groove across the rampart, and through this the water began to flow.

As it flowed so it widened and deepened the channel and its level began to fall. Eve watched, expecting at any moment to see treetops and hilltops reappear. Eagerly she scanned the receding waters for the first signs of life. Something ruffled the surface of the water and a moment later a brown island appeared and grew, then another and another. Brown, deserted, dead. No grass; only mud and stones. No trees; only tree stumps. No buildings; only little heaps of stones. And no living thing.

The last of the water drained away. Only a few stagnant pools remained. Over the entire surface no living thing was to be seen. And Eve knew then that the flood had not drowned a living world; it had closed the grave over a world already dead. And she should have left it that way.

*   *   *

In her second dream she was on an island and with her were a great crowd of people. There was frantic activity – sounds of hammering and much shouting – and Eve saw that the men were making an enormous boat. When the boat was ready it was hauled down to the water's edge and the water rose up and floated it off. The people gathered around, shouting and singing. Then the men, some carrying long poles of wood and others armed with swords and spears, climbed on board.

Eve tried to ask her neighbours what they were doing, but they seemed not to hear her. She guessed that the boat was to carry them to safety and that when the men were on board the women would follow. 'We must hurry,' she said. 'The water is rising fast.' But again they took no notice of her.

All the men were now in the boat and still the women stood on the shore, watching, waving and cheering. 'Quick, quick,' shouted Eve in desperation. But no words came out of her mouth. Slowly the boat moved away from the shore. The poles, beating the surface of the water, like the legs of some giant insect, carried it slowly on its way.

As it moved out across the water, Eve saw another boat appear from behind another island. The two boats converged and the shouting and cheering of the women lining the shore rose to a frenzy. Nearer and nearer they drew to each other and then with a tremendous crash they collided. And now there were men everywhere, surging up on deck, hurling themselves at each other, fighting and killing. The boats were breaking to pieces. Men were in the water. Men were clinging to bits of wreckage. And still they fought on.

And still the watching women, in ever greater frenzy, shouted and cheered and leapt up and down. 'Victory! Victory! Victory!' they yelled. And all the time the flood continued to rise. It was round their ankles, round their knees, round their waists. They took no notice. Still they cried, 'Victory! Victory!' until one by one, they lost their footing, slipped into the water and were carried away.

*   *   *

In Eve's third dream she was walking through her beloved valley and it was springtime. She was on her way home and had just reached the avenue. She was alone, but on either side, between the trees, was a vast gathering of people, men and women and children together with many other creatures. And all around her in the air were strange and very wonderful sounds. These sounds, tangible almost as water, swept round her and lifted her up and carried her forward. Slowly and in great splendour and majesty they carried her down the avenue.

At the far end was the giant oak, its small leaves and flower tassels now radiant in yellow-green. They came to the oak and the people and the other creatures were around her and the sounds, ever louder, ever more thrilling, coursed through her entire body and seized her and lifted her up and placed her high in the branches of the oak. She looked down and the people turned their faces up to her, and among them she saw Adam. 'Adam,' she cried, fearing he hadn't noticed her. 'Adam, look upwards.' Their eyes met and they laughed.

For a while she continued to lie stretched out on the bed that she had made for herself, while dream and reality wrestled with each other. Then quite suddenly she saw what she must do. Indeed there was no alternative. She must return to Eden. Just possibly at the far end of the plain (for the plain must surely have an end) there might be survivors who, like herself, were now clinging to the rim of their world. Just possibly some man somewhere would find a way of surviving the flood. But she and they were separated by an ocean of water and neither could ever know of or come to the help of the other. Those others would have to go on to whatever lay on the far side. She could only go back.

So back she would go. Back through the mountains – if she could find her way – back to the forest where Adam had hunted, back to the garden where they had once lived together so happily. There would be no Adam, and she was now very old. But the Lord God might still be there and he might take pity on her and look after her and clothe her and feed her in her old age.

She went to the mouth of her cave and looked out. The rain had slackened but the prospect was infinitely depressing. Yet if she could find no comfort in what she could see, in her ears she could still hear the wonderful sounds that had accompanied her third dream and this gave her both determination and strength.

She ate. Then she prepared herself for her journey, making

up a bundle of food, clothing and various implements she thought might be useful.

Finally, turning her back on the waters that had drowned her valley and the plain and all its inhabitants and all that she and Adam and their descendants had achieved, all the good and all the evil, she set her face to the mountain and began to climb.

She struggled on through the rest of that day until weariness and darkness overtook her. Then she found an overhanging rock and in the slight shelter that it offered she made herself as comfortable as she could. She was wet and cold and her bed was hard. She ate a little of the food she had brought and tried to close her eyes. But that night no sleep came.

The following morning she ate a little more, repacked her bundle and went on her way. The clouds were all round her and the rain streamed down her face. So she let her feet and her instinct be her guides. They guided her well, as, left to themselves, they often do. Towards midday the sky began to lighten and then to brighten and then quite suddenly she was through the cloud and into the sunshine and could see at last what lay ahead of her.

There were two mountain peaks quite near at hand, one on either side of her, and the skyline joining them hung in a curve. She directed her feet to the lowest point of this curve; and as she approached it and no other skyline appeared beyond it, so her hopes rose that perhaps this was the ridge that separated the two plains. She stumbled up the last few paces, tripped, fell, but was able to look over the top. Yes, indeed it was the top and Eden lay somewhere beneath her. But alas it was totally hidden in dense cloud.

She lay there for some moments, exhausted but triumphant, pressing the ground with her hands and her face while the sun warmed her back and the wind blew through her hair. Then she got to her feet and stretched herself towards the sky. Then she turned and looked behind her, half hoping, perhaps, to see that the flood waters had subsided.

Whatever had happened down there, nothing of it was visible. Cloud lay below her on both sides. But above her the sky was blue, one single expanse of blue arching over her two worlds. The sky reached down to her and was all around her; and she seemed to flow upwards to meet it. Again she stretched her arms into the air. She threw her head back and opened her mouth and filled her lungs; and a new and strange feeling flowed through her body.

She looked around her to find the exact point at which her path, having left the valley she had come from, began its descent into the valley ahead, the highest point in her journey. And there she stood; and once again everything everywhere – past, present and perhaps also future – became a part of her. She and the world became one.

Then she sat and unwrapped her bundle and laid her possessions out to dry. She was reluctant to begin her descent. It was so beautiful up here, so clean and pure. She divided her remaining food into two equal parts and very slowly she ate one of them. Then she lay down to rest.

A little finger of mist crept up the mountainside and chilled her. She opened her eyes. The sun was lower in the sky. She must be on her way.

She retied her bundle, picked up her stick and began her descent. Soon the sun vanished and the mist was once more all around her.

Somewhere along the bottom, out of sight, ran a little river and on the other side was the forest. If she crossed the river and followed the edge of the forest she would eventually come to the garden.

She reached the river in the late afternoon. She had heard it before she had seen it and it had filled her with alarm. The sight of it confirmed her fears, for it was now a broad and angry torrent.

Anxious to get across as quickly as possible, now that she was so near her journey's end, she stepped into the water and moved out over the smooth stones. A few paces from the bank she lost sight of her feet in the brown and foaming water. She grasped her stick in both hands and moved more cautiously, feeling with her stick, using it as a support, and then sliding her feet. The water was not deep but it pulled strongly round her legs and the stones were slippery. Once she nearly lost her balance. After a while she looked back to see how far she had come. Alas, it was only a tiny distance. She returned to the shore. If she were ever to reach the other side she must choose the best possible place and then abandon her belongings. All that she had brought with her except her stick must be left behind.

She set off downstream and eventually decided on a spot where the very width of the river led her to hope it might also be shallow. She undressed and, taking her stick, moved into the water a second time.

The far bank was lined with trees which were grey and dim in the misty rain. The wind blew and shook their branches. Eve stood knee deep in the water looking across. What a distance had yet to be covered! Suddenly she saw someone on the other side waving to her. It was Adam.

'Adam,' she cried in amazement. 'How did *you* get there?'

A wild surge of hope swept over her. Adam had gone on ahead of her and was waiting for her! Now surely she would get across. If she slipped and fell he would come to her rescue. With new confidence she moved further out and the water tugged at her thighs.

When she looked up again he had vanished. No. There he was, waving still. The wind came and the branches waved more wildly . . . and Adam dissolved. Two moving branches

and a tree trunk: that was all it had ever been. For a moment hope was drowned in despair.

But of course it could not have been Adam. Adam was long ago dead. . . . Yet perhaps, though he was dead, something of him still lived and was over there waiting for her, calling to her, urging her not to give up. Perhaps he had been trying to point to her the best way across. Which way had he been pointing? She looked up again. The branches waved. That way! That way!

The wind was all about her. The rain stung her face, almost, blinding her. The torrent roared. And through it and in it she heard once again the noble music of her third dream, and it lifted her up and sustained her and gave her strength.

'Adam!' she cried out. 'Wait for me. I'm coming!' She threw away her stick and in perfect confidence she turned and faced the water and leant against it, facing upstream and moving sideways.

The water rose and flung its arms around her waist and the great chords of the music crashed in her ears. . . .

AFTERWORD

NOAH survived. Will Eve?

Noah's flood was an act of God. Yet in a sense it was an act of man, for it was man's wickedness that brought down on him God's punishment. Eve's flood was more directly an act of man. Yet man may well reply that it was in a sense an act of God: the inevitable result of his following God's instructions to subdue and rule the world. His immense success contained the seeds of ultimate disaster.

The fiercer the fire the sooner it burns itself out. Perhaps from the ashes of the age of Adam will arise a new age, the age of Eve, an age in which her feelings for the world – so different from his – will dominate human conduct.

Eve, attempting to get back across the river, is forced to abandon all the artifices man has devised. She takes with her something that she herself is scarcely aware of. Indeed she has no word to describe it. But it gives her the determination to make that fearful journey, and, if she succeeds, it will be one thing that the new age can safely inherit from the old, one wholly noble and benevolent achievement. Music.